Edith L. Winn

Cadences

Edith L. Winn

Cadences

ISBN/EAN: 9783337380809

Printed in Europe, USA, Canada, Australia, Japan

Cover: Foto ©Andreas Hilbeck / pixelio.de

More available books at **www.hansebooks.com**

CADENCES

By
EDITH LYNWOOD WINN

BUFFALO
CHARLES WELLS MOULTON
MDCCCXCVIII

To Old Friends.

Each year to ancient friendships adds a ring,
As to an oak, and, precious more and more,
Without deservingness or help of ours,
They grow, and, silent, wider spread, each year;
Their unbought ring of shelter or of shade.
Sacred to me the lichens on the bark,
Which Nature's milliners would scrape away;
Most dear and sacred every withered limb!
'Tis good to set them early, for our faith
Pines as we age, and, after wrinkles come,
Few plant, but water dead ones with vain tears.

—James Russell Lowell.

CONTENTS

PREFACE.

EDITH Lynwood Winn was born in Foxboro, Mass., a suburb of Boston. Her early life was spent in the public schools of her native town. She was graduated from the High School, the youngest member of her class, when scarcely seventeen years of age.

She then entered the Framingham, Mass., State Normal School, from which institution she was graduated in her nineteenth year, one of the youngest members of a large class. She then assumed the duties of teacher of history and methods in Fairfield Military Academy, Fairfield, New York, where she remained two years. She had played the violin since her childhood, and had received some instruction. Her love for her chosen instrument became so great that she resigned her position at Fairfield and went to Boston, where, for about nine months, she was the pupil of Julius Eichberg, then director of the Boston Conservatory. During this time she held the position of teacher in the schools of Medfield, Mass., it being a rule in that State that all Normal graduates should teach at least one year in the public schools of the State.

Her health failing, she was obliged the following year to accept a position in the South at Shorter College, Rome, Ga., where she taught Latin and algebra and had a few pupils on the violin, mandolin and guitar. Her health being completely restored, on the following year she accepted the position of teacher of violin and history in Beaver College at Beaver, Pa. From this time she began to give her whole attention to music. She studied voice and later the violin during the summer season with Bernhard Listeman of Chicago.

She accepted the position of non-resident teacher of stringed instruments in Beaver, Geneva and Westminster Colleges. She determined to devote herself to music alone and to better prepare herself for that work. She received a leave of absence for one year, which she spent in Berlin as a pupil of Prof. Johann Kruse, of the celebrated Joachim Quartette. While in Berlin she wrote constantly, being a correspondent for the "Etude," "Musician," "Music" and other well-known magazines. Her health again breaking down she was obliged to spend the summer in Pommern, one of the northern provinces of Germany. In September she returned to America, where she has been constantly teaching and giving concerts and lectures on music and on life in Germany. She has made a tour of Eastern Massachusetts, Western New York and Western Pennsylvania this year, but she has given much time to teaching. Her poems, "Cadences," will be followed by a novel —"Berolina," dealing with music-life abroad. While Miss Winn regrets that she has not given her whole time to the cultivation of one gift, she believes that there is a verse which reads for her and will ever spur her on, "Whatsoever thy hand findeth to do, do it."

Cadences

THE TRANSFIGURATION OF A STRA-DIVARIUS.

From "Berolina—A Novel."

I.

FAR back in the sixteenth century,
There stood a mighty forest tree
In Southern Tyrol—so they say—
Where nought but saplings grow today.
This sturdy pine had much to do
With me. I'm recondite. Are you?

II.

Ah Tyrol! Now no more you vaunt,
Those mighty timbers resonant.
Acoustic properties? My soul!
Your saplings, non-commissioned, stole
Of priests that stately forests stood,
Are not of Stradivarius blood.

III.

That forest tree of which I spoke
Is part of me, (I make no joke.)

'Twas felled by woodman's axe and sent
To fair Cremona, whence it went
To swell her annual timber feast—
That fine old pine, my quondam priest.

IV.

Beneath the sun, all seasoned fine,
Anon we lay—fair woods—some pine.
Our powers vibrational for art
These master makers knew by heart,
By weight, by sight, by all the aid
That keen and studied choice had made.

V.

A dainty strip—another so—
The master shot with long knife blow
Off from the body of the tree,
Close fibred as with sympathy.
He passed my pine, saw dozens more,
Quick tested them, rejected o'er
And o'er again—came back at last
To choose but me, to hold me fast.

VI.

Well, pine then part of miracle
Of wood, so indestructible
That old and marred—yes, all apart—
It could again be new by art;

Its joints repaired, its ribs made strong,
Its tail-piece new, its neck along—
Became a violin, in fine,
Grand Pattern Strad—say number nine.

VII.

Long, long within the shop I dwelt.
My master oft my pulses felt,
And softly o'er the trembling strings
Drew bow, till air seemed full of wings.

IX.

Said he one day, "Me you must leave."
Then musing, "Filippo doth grieve."
That day there came a dark-haired man,
Hard-featured, sullen, swart with tan;
Me he adored, allegiance—crazed;
My tones he heard, half-awed, amazed.
There in that dusky shop, half hid
By the church of St. Dominic, he did
Such magic draw with bow and string
That e'en my master's mind took wing;
So that he left his work beloved,
A thing in many years unproved;
For master neither thought of men,
Nor politics, nor siege,—and when
He slept—that workman consummate—
None knew, nor when he talked nor ate.

X.

I see him yet, nor man nor boy,
A wizard-like, white-capped envoy
With leather apron on awry,
Accoutred low, in genius high;
His mind so bent on seeking Truth,
'Twas said he never had known youth;
His trade his life, his world his own,
Incomparable he stood alone.
'Twas so I knew him centuries back —
Great Stradivarius, alack,
Worn out with secrets precious pent,
When I was on my mission sent.

XI.

Forgive diversion. So I went
With lofty aim and mind intent
To bless the world. I heard the gold.
Filippo paid the price, I'm told,—
Filippo, man of dusky hue,
Friend of my master—as men true.

XII.

He played Adagios—weird strains—
Vivace when the tempo gains,
Then presto with a hundred trills,
And double stops in shivering thrills

With death-like madness, till his breath
Came thick and fast—nor life nor death
Was in his face—fortissimo
Shrieked strings to bow!
Then changed his mood.   But whispered he
A dream of Southern, quiet sea
Sun-kissed in summer, redolent
With blossoms of the Orient.
'Twas witchery!   They smiled who wept,
As genius fathoms-deep yclept
Confronted them.   Some saw aright—
A human soul cried out for light!

XIII.

That wiry man with deep set eyes
Had fathomed all the mysteries,
Depths of all passions, which have slept
In calmer men, have outward crept
Alone in men of life intense,
Who've lost the star of hope and sense.

XIV.

Yet he had caught a glimpse of heaven
One day.   His heart was leaven!
He loved a woman—him she feared;
He lost her—friends but laughed or jeered;

Temptations came when love was lost.
His heart went into music.   Frost
Came mingling with his raven hair—
Well, woman's loss made foul of fair.

XV.

'Twere well for him he loved his art;
He lived in it, 'twas his apart,
Weird music of aonther world;
Strange vistas oft before him whirled.
Men heard, amazed, these mysteries,
These supernatural elegies,
The discourse of a maestro,
And called him wizard here below.
God knows the heart of man and he
Sees in each life nobility;
The frail deplores, the good commends,
The genius knows—its noble ends.
Men are but creatures, twisted, bent
It maybe,—of environment.
I know that God spoke in the man,
Through passion mantling cheek of tan.
No struggle without peerage there,
No effort without half-said prayer,
No sympathy without Christ-like soul,
Dwarfed, it is true.   Man is but mole.

XVI.

Time passed. The man that smiles or tears
Drew at his will, mid loudest cheers,
All Vulcan-spent, laid down his life.
Death disenthralled, all doubt and strife
Were naught to him—Italia's own.
I, his heart's love, was left alone.

XVII.

I dwelt again in shop—years passed;
My value grew—importance vast;
At last there came a buyer grand,
With tawny beard and soft white hand,
An amateur with pounds to spare;
Heaven help me, how his eyes did stare!
He felt my back and graceful neck;
He drew some frigid tones, a check
To throbbing heart and sensitive.
A Strad. rebelled. I would not live
A victim to such passion-lack!
I in a year to shop came back.
My bridge had fallen, sound-post too—
My master tired—wished something new.

XVIII.

In time on me a new sun shone.
My gloom was joy, my night was morn.

A Belgian, famed for wondrous skill,
My hidden charms awoke at will.
My slumbering senses stirred. He pressed
Me, held me, soft caressed
Till I gave out my heart, my life,
To him, my Belgian—I his wife!

XIX.

There is methinks in Music's sway
A thing to poison one today,
Tomorrow, recreate and bless;
One's moods are strange, I do confess.
You know that Beethoven D dur?
As it your wakening sense doth lure,
Your'e gay. The Schubert then in G?
Ah Heaven, you're sad! Heart o'er the sea!
From concert you go a better man.
Who says God spoke not? 'Tis his plan
Through art and music to control
The longings of the human soul.
O Civilizer of the human race—
Music!—but Strad. must have its place.

XX.

To Belgium, happy, went I then,
My virtuoso drawing men

By cunning technique, breadth of tone,
By high conception—I alone
Responding to his soul, through wood
With human instinct half-imbued.

XXI.

Some time went by.   He died, this love.
God took him, men do say—above.
My soul then pined for years.   I grieved.
My power yet good, my gloss retrieved,
I dwelt in case of glass.   I slept.
One day, in German shop, I wept
At last to feel my neck soft pressed
By hand of love.   A man possessed
With passion's fire and lofty aim,
Nor yet unskilled, nor yet to fame
Wide-known, well-loved me—that I felt;
Like blushing maid, a Strad. can melt
By word of love, by touch of hand,
Can melt in pity—'twas so planned.
My soul sang, strings sang, bow sang loud.
My Rhapsody drew forth a crowd
Of lazy loiterers, within
The storehouse of my kith and kin—
The shop.   I felt his fingers rest,
As lover when he first has pressed

The hand he hopes one day to own,
To safe install in his heart's throne.
He played first softly—'twas a strain
Of deepest longing mixed with pain!
He touched his trembling lips half-sad
To neck of mine.   It made me glad!

XXII.

I throbbed so he was not unmoved.
He touched my strings again and proved
My sweetness.   Romanze—Rubinstein
He played— E major, half-divine!
I felt his power.   I broke at will
Into ecstatic, holy thrill!
He paused.   He could not stand, for nerves.
Well, he was human and that swerves.
He loved me,—be it good or bad
He'd sell his all to have a Strad.
He took me—that's enough.   That day
I went with him in case so gay
Of yellow leather, reverend,
The world my home—this man my friend.
Describe him?   He was tall and strong,
His hair soft brown, his eyes like song;
His mouth like woman's sensitive
Yet firm; his heart like sieve

When friend had need.   His name—my boy?
His name?   I speak it softly, coy—
Otto Von Cranach, Prince not he
Save by innate nobility;
His armor Truth, his weapon bow,
His cause Humanity's wild throe.

XXIII.

That day young Otto quite beside
Himself, with manly pride
Addressed me: "You're a wondrous prize,"
Said he, "Ah, you shall see his eyes,
Joachim's, when I hold to view
Your lovely form and play on you!
His ecstasy I see—I know.
Now can I see his two eyes glow!"

XXIV.

Then Otto sought his teacher straight.
Eternal youth hath genius.   Great
Joachim came—could not refuse
My boy, and straightway did enthuse
Me—thing of wood—that glorious day!
I've ne'er recovered from his sway.
He patted Otto's shoulder too,
And said: "I hope great things for you,

My boy.   Guard well your Strad.''
I thought with joy my boy'd go mad!

XXV.

Time passed, he loving only me,
Developed virtuousity.
One day (shall I that time forget?)
My Otto seemed quite changed, and yet
His genius broader grew each day.
I felt his thoughts, though, far away.
He loved.   I knew it, felt its thrill!
'Twere better so.   *She* felt my will.
They played together Bach, Godard—
(Duets for violins).   He starred.
She taught him how to breath out love
In beatific strains that move.
Sometimes she sat, now red, now pale,
Unnerved, despairing, (woman's frail)
And then anon quite strangely gay
She talked to while the time away,
But watching Otto's stolen glance.
'Twas so they dwelt in Love's young trance.

XXVI.

That could not last.   The climax came.
She promised, well—she'd take his name.

O, highly gifted, noble man!
Dear God, why changed you all the plan?
They could not marry.   It seems best.
Love such as their's oft kills.   Her breast
Had pain enough to move the skies
When she had made the sacrifice!
I know not—some wild ricochet
Shot through his frame.   I, laid away,
Heard smothered groan and wild appeal,
Then shrieks that made my blood congeal.
'Twas yesterday.   Oh, pain and woe
Rack my poor body.   He lies low!
My strings cry out, and throbbing wood
Seem as a thing with sense imbued.
I feel his hand—his dying hand,
I hear his feeble half-command.
My neck doth feel an iron will
In touch of clammy hand.   A thrill
Comes 'er me!   All is mystical.
My Otto lies (I feel it all)
On bed of death!   I see *her* there.
No orange flower will crown her hair.
My darling hears my last reveille,
His requiem.   He starts up, pale,
And strikes me once—his hand like ice.
I know not why I crash in trice.

Cadences

My sound-post goes, my bass-bar too!
Otto is dead!   A master new
For me?   Nay, I die!   God, let in
My soul!   A Strad. hath nought of sin.

BERLIN, November, 1896.

DER DROSCHKEN-KUTSCHER.

I SAW him sitting at his post,
    'Twas on a bleak December day,
    Close on to Christmas I may say—
Before I heard the New Year's "Pros't."

He was a sorry sight—unkempt,
    Too tipsy-rubicund, asleep
    Or meditating. . . . Skies that weep
As often as Berlin's, men tempt.

The *restauration* is near,
    And round the corner a *bier halle;*
    'Tis warm and bright on a winter's day,
And nights there's dancing, singing, cheer.

A poor old *kutscher's* not more weak
    Than he who sits in smart dress-suit
    Within the *droschke,* drunk to boot,—
A saturant with champagne-beak.

Ah no, for many's the time my swell
    The droschken-kutscher's brought you home,
    When you would from *gesellschaft* roam—
A trifle much too gay—You laugh?

Well, well, the *kutscher* has a heart.
His *frau* knows—so do I. His *frau*
Lives in a *keller*. Children now?
Three boys—one dead. My quick tears start!

One day she came not. I employed
The *kutscher's frau*. I was sore tried—
Was going on a journey wide—
Her long delay me quite annoyed.

I knew the *kutscher's* number well—
Four hundred six his cab had said;
I found him at the corner—head
Bowed like a reed, he sat. Rain fell.

I thought him glum—did him abuse—
Asked sharply for his tardy *frau*.
He came down from his box. . . Ah, now
I see him in his monstrous shoes.

I see his blue coat, seedy hat,
His yellow collar—but his eyes
I never shall forget. Surprise
Upon my careless visage sat—

Surprise and pity. Not a word
The *droschen-kutscher* spoke to me.
We drove away. I felt not free
To question—curious, that deferred.

We drove into a narrow street,
  So full of children, and of noise
  That I was deaf. A crowd of boys,
Knapsacks on backs, from school ran fleet.

The *kutscher* opened wide a door—
  It was his humble *keller*. There
  A woman stood. . . He touched her hair
And whispered, *"Mutter,"*—nothing more.

The harsh rebuke, the petty whim,
  I had it in my mind to speak,
  Died on my lips. . . . This mother meek,
Like a wounded deer ne'er smiled on him—

Ne'er smiled on him, ne'er smiled on me,
  But, pointing to unfinished work,
  (Her ironing-board)—she sent a dirk
Down to my heart of sympathy.

Then, turning, beckoned she to me
  Where, in a tiny room beyond,
  I entered, unprepared, unwarned. . . .
She bade me something touch and see.

"Mein Kind!" she sobbed and shook like leaf—
  I stepped beside a bed to raise
  The coverlet. . . . A waxen face,
A child's dead face, explained Loves grief.

I kissed the little face and then
  I took the mother by the hand.
  I talked upon the Spirit Land—
The Land beyond our grief and ken.

And then we went back to the board,
  Where lay the robe so clean and fair
  The child should in its coffin wear;
('Twas all the mother could afford.)

I dropped a gold-piece on the hearth.
  Next day a wreath I sent beside.
  That was not all. . . . At eventide
I prayed for women who on earth

Have lived and loved and struggled sore,
  Have had deep griefs too hard to bear. .
  Who takes no Cross no Crown shall wear.
To love the poor's to love God more.

POMMERN, June, 1897.

WOMAN, WHY WEEPEST THOU.

WOMAN, why weepest thou?   Thy son
        still lives.
        Yes, God is good.   He taketh, yet He
        gives.
He picks the fairest and most precious flowers.
His was the gift.   The care of it but ours.

Woman, why weepest thou?   Thy son's rich
        store
Of knowlede lives.   Wouldst thou ask more?
Doth not the Holy Book now speak new things
To thee?   What comfort, too, it brings.

Woman, why weepest thou?   But look around
Where childless, yearning women oft are found
Alone.   And see'st thou not their hidden woe?
They have not known thy joy below.

Thine was a boon, when to thy throbbing breast
He nestled every night to rest,
Thy child, and later at thy knee
Learned from his books half-mastered mystery.

Thine was the boon, too, when in later years
Came he and brushed thy fair hair back
    through tears,
And, half-ashamed to be a boy again,
He told thee secrets in the old, old strain.

And then when he had chosen to obey
The call to serve his fellow men, thy yea
Was a benediction, as thou smiled
Approval, thanking God for child.

Out from his books there came a solemn voice:
"Thou, son, in fairer fields shalt be my choice.
Out from the garden of the Lord
I call thee home to minister to God."

Then with a high, sweet smile, O mother blest,
Thy eldest, precious child, went home to rest.
Look through thy tears and proudly raise thy
    head—
God, passing others, chose *thy* son instead.

Jan. 16, 1898.

JOHN BRADLEY'S WIFE.

COME a little closer, John.
　　Draw me to the window-sill,
Ere the sun has once more gone
　　Down behind the Chestnut Hill.

Wrap me warmer, John, 'tis Spring
　　And the cold affects me sore,
Since the cough grew worse.　Oh bring
　　That old shawl, the one I wore—
That I wore, John, years ago
　　When we walked o'er Chestnut Hill,
Both with footsteps strangely slow,
　　Past your father's house and mill.
This old shawl was new then, John;
　　I was but eighteen, you say,
Yes, and rosy-cheeked.　You laugh?
　　I was but a child that day.

I remember how you stole
　　Your young arm about my waist,
As upon a grassy knoll
　　You and I sat, modest-faced.

"Nay," I could not say, dear John;
  You then took my willing hand,
Drew me to you. I like fawn
  Gayly sprang away. You planned.

Sprang you from the grassy knoll,
  Seized me by my gingham dress,
Bade me answer on my soul
  What I dared not half confess.
"But the dew is falling, John,"
  I replied, as though I heard
Not a word you spoke, my John;
  (Women oft defer the word.)
Then you saw the warm, bright glow
  Of the evening sun upon
My young cheek. You caught me—Oh
  And you kissed till day was gone!

The sun kissed the west,
  The dew kissed the flower,
A youth kissed a maid—
  Oh for Love's power;

Forty years have passed, dear John,
  Since our happy wedding day.
In the village church, my John,
  Father's hand gave me away.

Cadences

I can see my muslin gown,
  And my apple blossoms, too,
Which the children of the town
  Over my light bride veil threw,
And beneath my bride feet strewed—
  It was in the early Spring.
One year from betrothal viewed
  I my golden wedding ring.
In the twilight, John, that night,
  Wandered we upon the hill,
From our guests quite out of sight;
  And we sat beside the mill.

Of the future, shy, we spoke—
  My housewifely lore, your skill
With the mill and farm.   Awoke
  My young heart in proud wife-thrill.

"Little wife," you said, (The moon
  Saw a kiss upon my face)
"God bless you!   We must too soon
  With our guests resume our place."

The moon kissed the river,
  The child kissed the flower,
Clouds came and the winter—
  Oh for Love's power!

Come a little closer, John,
　It is growing darker.　Day
Has all vanished; night forlorn,
　Night of life comes.　John, but lay
Your gray head upon my breast.
　Do you hear my fond heart beat?
I must soon have rest—long rest—
　To be near you is so sweet.

Something strange I will confess:
　John, do you remember here
Where I stood in bridal dress
　On our wedding night of cheer?
Yes?　The light was in my heart.
　Three years later, one gray day
In the early Fall, (you start!)
　God took all the light away.

John, she lay—my babe, my first,
　In this room—(Hush, I will speak)
And, when I had heard the worst,
　With an awful, awful shriek
I fell prostrate on her form.
　From my body young and strong
Life and love—Oh love so warm—
　Breathed I on her, sobbing long.

Then you took me from her side,
   Once again upon my cheek
Pressed a kiss. I Heaven decried—
   Raved and raved till I was weak.
Well, we laid her then away—
   Little Mary, first and last.
We have lived alone. I pray
   Not another wife may fast
For the love, the bounteous love,
   Of a little welcome child,
Wafted from the world above,
   Angel-winged and angel-smiled.

The sun kissed the lily,
   It lived for an hour.
Life cometh and goeth—
   Oh for Love's power!

John, the rosy sun is setting
   Down behind old Chestnut Hill.
"Long ago?" . . . The cow-bell ringing
   Was that or the whip-poor-will?

Why, you kiss my shawl, my finger,
   And my hand is wet, dear boy! . . .
"Not since Mary died?" . . . You linger
   On the words, "our child, our joy."

You have not been loving, tender?
  Nonsense, John, your brain's not right.
Listen! Draw me near the fender . . . .
  Ah, the air is chill tonight.

John, you say your "heart grew colder—
  Farming, politics, coal mine?"
Ah, your cares have made you older.
  Grief has aged me, made me pine.

I was lonely for my Mary,
  But I never spoke, dear John;
Life was ever, ever dreary,
  After all its hope was gone.

I was not, dear John, a true wife.
  I should not have mourned so sore.
God rebuked me, saw my grief-life;
  My rebellion no child bore.

All these years, my John, we've prospered;
  We are rich, the neighbors say.
We have acres—gold—you're honored—
  Yes, you're Congressman today.

How you press my hand! I'm colder . . .
  John, the brandy and the air! . . .
There, that's better. We are older
  Than we were that Springtime fair.

When with blossoms—God—I'm dreaming.
  John, what say you love, "Forgive"?
What have I to pardon, seeming
  Only half a wife to live?

Only half a wife, John Bradley,
  Yet I loved you day and night.
John, no heart ere beat so gladly
  Nor so proudly as that night
Mine beat, when from town and county
  Came your friends, and at our door
Offered they their praise, their bounty,
  Honor and their trust in store.
"Cheers for John, our own John Bradley!
  "Going to Congress!" "Heard the news?"
"News"? said you, as laughing gladly,
You declared you would refuse.

Then you came to me bedridden,
  As I lay here, ears quick-tuned
To the words that you were bidden
  To accept the post.   Communed
We then, John, as not for long years.   Oh
  Then you pressed a welcome kiss
On my lips.   I longed so for it!
  John, was anything amiss
All these years?—Yes? you "grew worldly"
  And you say, "Forgive, forgive!" . . .

God, forgive thine own handmaiden
  Who has called thee oft unjust—
God, is love, John . . . Meet me laden
  With the fruits of public trust.

Meet me, John, in Heaven—I'm dying!
  Meet me—We will talk it o'er
On the other side, where sighing
  Vanishes in spirit-lore.

The sun kissed a snow-flake,
  A man kissed a flower,
A dead apple blossom—
  Oh for Love's power!

John Bradley sat with bent, gray head
  Beside a pillow wet with tears.
"Oh that I could have died instead,"
  He said, "or bring back vanished years."
John Bradley ne'er to Congress went.
  Men said he mourned his wife. He knew
How deep remorse in shaft is sent,
  When Death's sting touches lives untrue.

The sun kissed a gray head,
  Which bent for an hour
O'er a grave on the hill-side—
  Oh for Love's power!

POMMERN, July, 1897.

HYMN.

The following Christian Endeavor hymn comes to us all the way from Berlin. It was written by Edith Winn, of the Berlin Christian Endeavor Society.— *Golden Rule, Boston.*

I.

PILOT, who across the ocean
   Guided us, thy pilgrim band,
    Shielded us from storm and tempest
    In the hollow of thy hand,
Guide us, band of earnest seekers,
   Guide us to the truth and light;
We are pledged to do thee service,
   Train our hearts and minds aright.

II.

Pilot, we would be a beacon
   In the world so full of sin,
A revolving light to others,
   Light reflecting, light within.
Pilot, draw us closer, nearer,
   We are very far from home.
Bless our dear ones o'er the ocean.
   Bless us as we wider roam.

III.

Pilot, make us valiant sailors,
    Loyal first to thy command;
Heart and intellect in service,
    True to God and native land.
Pilot, signal in the darkness
    To the Ships of nations, tossed
On the sea of Doubt or Error,
    Hail our brothers ere they're lost.

IV.

O the day, the glad day hasten,
    When our banner shall be known
From the Indies to the Arctic,
    From the hut to monarch's throne.
O the day, the glad day hasten,
    Of the brotherhood of man,
And the triumph of the Gospel,—
    God's most perfect, holy plan.

MAR., 1897.

A NEW ENGLAND VILLAGE, 1879.

From Janet's Diary.

WHEN the evening lamp is lighted,
    And the supper cleared away,
      In our wide old farm-house kitchen
        There is joy more than by day;
For, my father, feet in slippers,
    You sit puffing curly wreaths
From your pipe of clay, and softly
    Talk to yellow Tab, who breathes
With a sage delight in purring,
    As his back you soft caress,
While with other hand you fondle
    Me and compliment my dress.

Mother sits at table mending;
    Brother plays with tops and balls,
Or he takes a ride on horseback,
    Till from rocking-horse he falls.
Now you sit and talk of weather,
    Grandpa with his almanac,
Or you read aloud the Herald—
    Politics—baseball—the track.

Brother plays make wooden houses
   With his blocks. I read alway,—
Dickens some and Hawthorne also,
   Wondrous tales (too old, you say)
Wondrous fairy tales in English,
   Grimm's and Anderson's, and then
Little Women—all of Alcott
   Not forgetting Little Men.
How the time flies, till at signal
   Mother's black eyes dance and gleam.
She is conscious what is coming,
   Little mother at her seam.
Yes, tis coming from the bed-room,
   Well worn case with battered side,
Quaint sarcophagus of pine wood—
   Nightly solace—father's pride.
Ah, within its sacred lid there
   Lies a thing of wood so dear
That my father's eyes grow brighter,
   Younger he by twenty year;
And the sight of that old fiddle
   Makes dear grandpa boy again.
Out it comes and then the tuning.
   D sobs, A wails, E rasps—then
Comes a struggle with the G string—

See saw, see saw, shiver, wail,—
Father holding bow like hammer,
   With his chin to fiddle's tail.
Then from bed-room I, quite bashful,
   Bring my little violin,
Seat myself at father's elbow,
   Neck to neck and chin to chin.
Long we sit and play together
   Blue-backed "Winner's old Duets,"
Reels and Jigs and country dances
   (Minus dancers)—well-worn pets.
Sometimes little brother helps us
   With his shrill-toned flageolet,
Till his eyes go drooping softly;
   Bed claims him—we're left duet.
Nine, the old clock in the corner,
   High old relic of our race,
Strikes, its pendulum slow moving;
   With its stroke to bed—best place.
Clock, I feel the nightly picture
   Without you were not complete,
As I give one look behind me,
   Ere to bed I softly creep.

BOSTON, 1885.

Years have passed—Another picture:
   Grandpa's laid at rest.   Alone

43

By the evening lamp my parents
  Muse. The fiddle gives but moan.
Good night father, good night mother,
  Good night childhood, glorious, free;
Welcome larger growth, my fiddle,
  In Conservatory we!
Ere I turn Life's pages over,
  Dear God, keep the childhood bright,
Keep the purity and home love,
  Help me aye to live aright!

BERLIN, 1890.

Swift hegira, Time, fly backwards,
  Evanescent dream, more clear
Strike my clouded, half-dim retina;
  Come back home-land, youth and cheer.
I am tired, alone and friendless,
  Weary with the noise and din,
Of a heartless, foreign city;
  I am mutable within.
What care I for worldly praises,
  Sycophantine words unfelt?
New friends never speak as old ones,
  Souls don't meet and hearts don't melt.
Oh, I must recall youth's pictures,
  Though they're never more the same,

Cadences

Never more can impulse give me,
　Having nought to do with fame.
E'en the glow upon the hill top,
　By my father's farm-house door,
Seemed last year to 've lost its splendor;
　Sunset too no radiance wore;
All the beauty of the elm-trees
　Seemed so common to me, too;
I was restless and ambitious,
　Having larger things in view.
There were scars upon the landscape,
　There were shadows on the hill,
There was soughing in the pine trees,
　When night came and all was still.
We were sitting in the kitchen.
　I was going o'er the sea.
Father sighed and mother whispered,
　"Sands shift for ETERNITY."
So I left them, sad yet hopeful,
　Thinking to come back some day,
Less a fiddler, more an artist—
　Now my heart's abandoné!
True there's beauty in these classics,
　Arbiter I am not yet.
Will the world of art be richer
　For my life?　No, habits fret.

Cadences

Do they make me any happier—
  Etude, jocund scherzo, gigue?
All offend me.   All are nettling,
  Have for me some vague intrigue.
Reveries and trembling Romanze,
  Largo much and Placido,
For my mood Midsummer Night's Dream—
  That beloved Notturno. .   .   .   .   .
So I wrote last night and *heute*
  I have heard an artist play.
Feats of skill that made the senses
  Reel astonished by his sway
Were as naught to me; I, famished,
  Heard but beauty, subtle, fine.
Then, all passion-roused by genius,
  Drank I in the glorious wine
Of that Rondo—G dur—Haydn,
  Then a Romanze—his own best.
Sympathy, God-given physician,
  Stilled the pain that racked my breast.
Hope he played and life and action,
  Love for every human thing.
So the artist preached my sermon,
  At his music care took wing.
Greatness caught my moody envy,
  Shamed it.   I bowed low to him.

Cadences

My scintilla from the artist
   Gave me purpose.   Past was whim.
His a grand, a high commission,
   Mine not less a call from God,
Call to make the world the richer
   By each daily act and word.
To my nobler self triumphant
   Played the artist one rich strain
That shall live with me forever—
   I am victor after pain.

BERLIN, October, 1896.

TO MISS C. G.

HAIL to thee, Hail to thee, child of a King!
God speaks in thee
Through sympathy.
Eternity—
Blest Trinity
Lent thee a Song, glorious Song to a King!

Music, thy soul's strongest instinct, we bless.
All who hear thee
Better must be;
Thou are so free,
Touching each key—
Magic in touch—a half-sensuous caress.

Woman, half child, true musician thou art,
Heart in thy tear,
Tone without fear;
God placed thee here—
He is oft near,
Seeking through music to touch the world's
Heart.

Cadences

—

Back through the ages thy soul had its birth.
      Thou, as a child,
      Felt it and smiled;
      Yes, thou so mild
      Blessed, ne'er defiled,
With thy sweet symphony, not of the earth.

What has been given thee, child of the South—
      Warm temperament,
      Sweetest content,
      Grave sentiment,
      Passion all lent—
Cherish it, nurture it, prayer in thy mouth.

Some day thou, standing before a white throne,
      Talents received,
      Losses retrieved,
      Sorrows relieved,
      Glory achieved—
All to the King must give back as His own!

BERLIN, May, 1897.

49

C. E. HYMN.

To the Y. P. S. C. E., Berlin, 1896.
Words by Edith Lynwood Winn.
Music by Isabella Beaton.

I.

LOVING God on Thee we call,
Thou to us art all in all.
Holy Saviour, Heavenly King,
Offerings to Thee we bring.

II.

When on earth Thy children meet,
Laying trophies at Thy feet,
Thou dost bless Thy pilgrim band,
Serving Thee in a foreign land.

III.

Thine the hand and Thine the brain,
Thine the heart we seek to train;
Thine the life we give to Thee,
Ere we crossed the stormy sea.

IV.

Take our talents, they are Thine;
Round our band Thy love entwine,

Love that knows no creed nor race,
So wide-reaching is its grace.

V.

Father, now Thy children here
From all lands are gathered near,
That they may but serve Thy plan
For the brotherhood of man.

VI.

As we pass on Life's highway,
May the word that we shall say
Be remembered in Thy love,
When Thy children meet above.

TO A FRIEND ON HER DEPARTURE
FOR INDIA.

I MET thee and passed thee on Life's broad
    highway;
I touched thy soft hand—an electric relay
      'Twixt my life and thine—
      No need to entwine
      Our fingers.   'T was day!

I looked in thine eye and beheld Truth and
    Love—
Thy blue eye, as blue as the Heavens above.
      Thine eye hath a Star;
      It came from afar—
      I saw it.   'T was day!

What is it I caught in thy gentle, sweet face,
In hand and in eye, in thy womanly grace?
      Thou'rt not an old friend;
      Our paths different trend.
      No matter.   'Tis day!

I need not to try thee, my friend of an hour;
The glance that I caught in thine eye gave me
    power.

Cadences

Our souls met and spoke—
Our pulses awoke.
I loved thee.   'Twas day!

God bless thee sweet sister, so soon complement
To him, whose existence less full and content,
 Less complete were alone;
 Twin souls, two-in-one
 Thou shalt be.   'Tis day!

Bon voyage alone to the Land of the Sun—
Fair India, Malaya, where dwells thy loved one.
 Safe passage my Star,
 Safe anchor afar.
 He greets thee.   'Tis day!

I see thee in vision, thy robe purest white,
Thy hair crowned with blossoms for Hymen
 bedight.
 His Star thy bright Sun,
 The day when made one
 At the altar.   'Tis day!

Long life to thee, sister, and ministry sweet.
I know not if ever on earth we shall meet,
 Again touching hand.
 Glad faith ours.   Bright land
 When life's over.   .   .   All's day!

BERLIN, May, 1897.

TO MISS S. M.

I.

I HAVE struggled with Life's problems,
  Like an agonist in quest
Of a prize so wondrous fashioned
  That its image brought unrest.
Striving vainly, something whispered,
  "Child, Whatever Is is Best."

I have struggled with ambition,
  Thought none should my mood molest,
Lest I lose the spark of power
  God had placed within my breast.
Failure came. Self shrank. God whispered,
  "Child, Whatever Is is Best."

Once I stood beside a pillow
  Which a weary head soft pressed;
As I stood, the restless motion
  Ceased. A spirit sank to rest.
'Twas a grey day in September—
  "Child, Whatever Is is Best."

Others, climbing mountains higher,
  Seem with wealth and honors blest.

Cadences

I have wealth beyond the mundane,
   And I wear no lordly crest.
All my wealth is found in friendships—
   "Child, Whatever Is is Best."

Friends are they who see the struggle,
   See the nobler side of quest,
In penumbra weep beside us,
   Eclipse over, share our Fest,—
Say in shadow and in sunshine;
   "Child, Whatever Is is Best."

I would gladly stay beside thee,
   In thy friendly, friendly nest,
But I go where duty calls me.
   Thou wouldst say, "With grief suppressed,
Learn to bear Life's burdens nobly—
   Child, Whatever Is is Best."

Doth it matter where we labor?
   To God's love we both attest.
Out upon Life's broad horizon,
   Heads bowed, we look toward the West,
There beholding in the sunset,
   "Child, Whatever Is is Best."

BERLIN, May, 1897.

EXTRACT FROM CLASS POEM.

Delivered at the Framingham State Normal School.
Forces for Truth.

TRUTH needs no color, she is clad
   In her own spotless loveliness.
  One knows her best who seeks her most,
   The world will yet her light possess.

Her radiance upon our way
  We must reflect from day to day,
Else rays are lost whose power might give
  Some soul an impetus to live.

Let us to self be true today,
  That higher self, God, known to thee.
Day serves not light more precious than
  A consecrated life can be.

The heart can be a royal throne;
  Let crowned Truth but dwell in thine,
And thou canst rule the mighty world—
  Since thou hast God and Truth divine!

TO BE OR NOT TO BE.

Class Poem—Foxboro High School.
Written at Sixteen Years of Age.

IN the midst of youthful dreamings,
  While our hearts from cares are free,
Comes to us a voice that sayeth:
  "Think! To Be or Not to Be."

Once it called our Nation's Fathers,
  And in time by efforts grand,
Waved the flag of Independence,
  Peace proclaiming o'er the land.

To another generation
  Came the voice: "Though you are free,
Blackened is your fair escutcheon
  By the curse of slavery."

"Freedom! shall it be or not be?"
  Shouted noble men and brave.
The Rebellion closed, and Freedom
  Blessed the soul of every slave.

As we meet the urgent question,
  We resolve to work with might
In life's widening field of effort,
  Battling ever for the right.

Cadences

How the myriad handed FUTURE
    Stretches out its shadowy palms,
Cheering onward, urging upward,
    Showing us a thousand charms!

Obvious duties are before us.
    Shall we idly turn away,
Putting off until tomorrow
    What we ought to do today?

Time lost is never found again,
    And fancied "time enough"
Soon bears one on from pleasures vain
    To fortunes hard and rough.

A coward's heart is that which fears
    The trial for some good,
Which falters throughout all its years,
    "I dare not though I would."

Constant toil all debts discharges.
    Sloth increases want and care
And, like rust, consumes much faster
    Than the hardest labors wear.

Youth is brief and time is fleeting.
    He who strives to reach the goal
Finds each passing moment precious,
    As the seasons onward roll.

He who works with steady purpose
Will not stop to question FATE
For he knows that small beginnings
Lead to issues truly great.

Stern experience only teaches:
They who learn to stand must fall.
Failures are but ways to winning,
If we follow Wisdom's call.

Disappointments are but rain-clouds
Sailing o'er the skies of LIFE,
Darkening for an hour only,
Bringing envy, grief and strife.

Brighter shall the welcome sun be
When the clouds have passed us by,
And the rainbow, Heaven's true promise,
Raises us to standards high.

One ray, at least of sunshine bright
Falls o'er a life most sad,
And cheers, supports and comforts
When the heart in gloom is clad.

Each one's future, like the Phœnix,
From the ashes of the past,
Wings its flight, and rises upward
To new heights, unknown and vast.

Perhaps we ne'er can reach the heights
  To which we long to rise;
We cannot all be first in fight,
  Nor all be great nor wise.

To mingle in the busy hum
  Of life, tho' sad or gay;
To think less of the ills to come,
  To labor more today;

To struggle onward in this sphere
  Until we find the true,
To gain in wisdom every year:
  This is for us to do.

What though we perish ere we reach
  The prize we would have won?
Tis surely much for every man
  To see good work begun.

Then let us aim to do our best,
  To have a purpose high,
Work out that purpose fearlessly
  And every foe defy.

Our labors are not reckoned less
  Because we fail to win.
Then let us toward the FUTURE press
  And on new tasks begin.

This motto let us not forsake,
    'Twill strength and courage lend;
'Twill put to flight all doubts and fears:
    "Look forward to the End."

    Look forward—you who fondly hope
        To make the END secure,
    Look upward too, and God will make
        Your progress safe and sure.

    And should you reach the mountain-tops
        Toward which Faith leads you on,
    And climbing, kind assistance lend
        To others faint and worn,—

    Then will your paths with others meet
        Upon the heights you see,
    Where you shall all together greet
        The vast Eternity.

AUF WIEDERSEHEN.

AUF Wiederschen, dear land toward which
    I've looked
    Since girlhood's years with yearnings fond
        and vague,
Believing that twixt me and thee a vast,
Unknown, impossible and ne'er to be
Dream-realized ocean gulf must be traversed,
Ere I could drink from out thy classic fount;
Believing that long years of steady toil
There needs must be, ere from my slender hoard
I dared to widen my horizon, and
Sail to my land of dreams at the expense
Of many golden pieces gained by wear
Of body, nerves and brain two-thirds collapsed;
Oh land of fondest dreams, fair Deutschland,
    —say,
What you have taught me that I did not know
    before!
One year with thee, one single soul-grown year,
Wherein I learned the vague uncertainty
Of living without compass fixed on one
Bright star that never changes its white light,—

The light that leads us to Life's highest goal:
(I then believed God stony that he made
Me wait upon His time to learn His will.)
One year in which I looked upon the skill
Of painters' hands, which have more deeply
    wrought
The story of men's lives than men themselves,
In those fine museums, where to rest awhile—
A day or two, a week or e'en a life,
Were but to see the world in miniature;
One year in which my daily, lightest task
Forbade a wish to peer into the life
About me, lest it might deter me from
My self-imposed seclusion with etudes.
Oh year, the fairest of the rose-leaved past,
My treasure year in Deutschland, goest thou
As other years into the umbra-past?
No, no thou cannot die, my aureole year,—
Thou cannot die, nor can thou ever lose
The freshness and the verdure of a time
When youth and hope vivacious bow the head,
As all the sterner tasks and sterner mould
Of womanhood begin to serious set
The features, and to knit the youthful frame
Together with the sinews of restraint,
Of patience and of hope and peace with God . .
What have I learned save music more to prize,

Cadences

Since I have learned it from the *Meister* hand
Of one in whom there lives and nobly rings
Such echoes from the Spirits of the past—
The wondrous beauty of Sebastian Bach,
The stately grandeur of a Beethoven,
The holy fire of Mendelssohn, the glow
Just vanished of a brother Brahms, beloved?
You know of whom I speak in words that fail—
Of great Joachim and his serious school.
'Twas in the labyrinth of strange, new truths
Of bowing and of phrasing, grounded fast
Into the satellites—those loyal men
Who long with him had studied—loved him
      too—
That I became myself a devotee
To all that was Joachim-like in thought.
I played from morn till night, and every glimpse
I caught of what seemed maze to me at first,
Enriched my nature, filled me with new zeal
To strive to conquer, and to feel in touch
With those emotions which, in truth, must
      spring
From deepest music-love intuitive,
Not taught in tricks of bow nor technic's skill.
And did I have this in my soul—this love
Of music and the power to voice desire?
No, I did not, but in the vague pursuit

Of that toward which my nature cried, I found
My heart to sympathy most deeply stirred,
Till all the world to me was brother—friend.
This then, in short, is what I learned, the while
I spent the bright gold-bits which I had saved,
Nor prized save that they spoke of toil God
    blessed
By trailing friendships in my labor's wake,—
This learned I, as all men may learn:
That what is in your soul will sing aloud;
It may not be in music nor in art,
It may not e'en be heard amid the crowd,
But what you take of beauty to your life
Will broaden it, and make it bear rich fruit
For time and for that larger cycle dim,
Whose end shall see us stand amid the throng
That press about the shining form of Him
Who made us one with Him by precious blood.
Then shall we learn what we have done on
    earth,
And how He treasured it in His rich store.

AUGUST 14, 1897, PASSING OUT OF THE ELBE

A GERMAN IDYL.

TWO dusty flowers bent forward mid the
 grain
 To catch a drop of dew,
 A "*guten morgen*," too,
For they were very friendly in the main.

Two lovers passed upon the broad *chaussee*,
 Marie, a peasant maid,
 And Hans, the gardener's aid,—
Two lovers who had kissed but once that day.

"O Hans," the maiden whispered, as she spied
 The *kaiserblume* blue,
 And the poppy, drinking dew,
"The flowers kissed while standing side by
 side."

Young Hans sprang down and, with a manly
 grace,
 He plucked the *kaiserblum'*;
 He plucked the sweet *mohnblum'*;
And touched each lightly to the maiden's face.

"Thou art," he said, "the fairest of all flowers,
  Thou *kaiserblume* blue;
  To thee I will be true
Until the day when we shall gladly wed."

"And thou, dear Hans," the maiden sweet
    replied,
  "Shalt be my poppy red,
  And thou shalt win me bread
With sweet *mohn* flavor full supplied."

He kissed her fair young cheek that brightly
    glowed,
  As down the broad *chaussee*
  They walked that August day,—
While two sweet flowers lay dying in the road.

POMMERN, Aug., 1897.

NOTE.—The *kaiserblume*, or corn-flower, is the national flower of Germany. It is said that Queen Louise, after her flight from Berlin, during its occupation by Napoleon, was, with her two children, journeying along a country road, on each side of which grew hundreds of corn-flowers amid the grain. The children were so delighted with the pretty flowers that they alighted from their carriage and picked a large bouquet for their beautiful Queen mother. From that time the corn-flower has been the national flower of Germany, since it was the wish of the Queen.

The *mohnblume*, or poppy flower, also grows in the grain fields. It is very fragile and a beautiful scarlet in color. The seeds of the flower are used in German biscuits, or *brotchen*, and are considered to be of fine flavor.

www.ingramcontent.com/pod-product-compliance
Lightning Source LLC
Chambersburg PA
CBHW021224260626
47172CB00002B/595